The Everglades

Mike Graf

Contents

The Everglades National Park

A Most Unusual Place

The Everglades National Park is in the United States of America (USA). It is at the southern tip of the state of Florida. It is a very unusual place. There are no mountains or hills. There are no canyons or valleys. Instead, the Everglades is a **grassland** with a very wide, slow-moving river flowing over and around it. There are also areas of forest, and waterholes filled with wildlife.

The Everglades is about 160 kilometres long and over 80 kilometres wide. Just north of the Everglades is Lake Okeechobee*. This lake is an important water source for the park.

* say *oh-ki-CHO-bi*

the Everglades from the air

About the Land and Water

As Earth warms and cools, ocean levels change. Southern Florida was above sea level during the ice age, when glaciers covered parts of Earth. But as the glaciers melted, the sea level rose and the ocean covered much of the Everglades area. Now, southern Florida is a flat grassland that is just above the water level. Underneath the water and grass is **limestone**.

Think and Talk About …

Most limestone is made up of the remains of marine creatures that lived millions of years ago.

The ground under the grass of the Everglades is limestone.

History of the Park

People lived in the Everglades for as many as 15 000 years before it became a national park. They hunted and fished there. When Europeans came in the sixteenth century, they had a devastating effect on the Native American communities in the area. Later, another group of Native Americans called the Seminole people moved to the Everglades, and their **descendants** still live in the area today.

In the early twentieth century, the government of Florida decided to drain the Everglades, so that the land could be farmed and developed. This destroyed the natural **habitat** of many animals in the Everglades. A journalist called Marjory Stoneman Douglas began to write about the need to protect the Everglades, and it was named a national park in 1947.

Think and Talk About ...

Marjory Stoneman Douglas was known as "the Mother of the Everglades".

a Seminole elder making a bow

Wet and Dry

The Everglades region has a **subtropical** climate. It has two **distinct** seasons. There is a warm, dry season and a warm, wet season. The wet season is very hot and **humid**. This attracts mosquitoes and other insects. It is often rainy, with thunderstorms and the occasional hurricane.

In the dry season, the weather is a little cooler. More people visit the park during the dry season.

Think and Talk About ...

Another name for the Everglades is *Pa-hay-okee*, which is a word in a Native American language that means “grassy waters”.

Plants of the Everglades

The Everglades has a very unusual **ecosystem**. The area is completely flat and just slightly above sea level. Salt water from the ocean flows into the Everglades and joins with fresh water coming from Lake Okeechobee.

Saw grass is the most common plant growing in the water of the Everglades. The Everglades is sometimes called a "sea of grass". But there are many other plants, including 25 kinds of orchids and over 125 kinds of trees. Mangrove trees grow at the southern end of the park, where the ocean tides meet fresh water coming from the north. Mangrove roots grow above the ground as well as below it.

Strangler fig trees are found on the small islands in the park. Their seeds start growing on other trees, and eventually strangle them. The gumbo-limbo is another species of tree that can be found in the Everglades. This tree has very distinctive reddish, peeling bark.

a gumbo-limbo tree

A strangler fig slowly strangles another tree.

Birds of the Everglades

The Everglades is well known as the home of a large variety of birds. Over 340 different kinds of birds can be spotted in the area. Flamingos, coots, ospreys, hawks, buntings, cormorants, egrets, falcons, storks, eagles, owls, cuckoos and other birds are often seen in the park.

The Everglades has a large number of **wading birds**. Wading birds have long legs that help them to move through shallow, muddy water. They nest in reedy areas or near ponds. Thousands of birds are known to nest in the Everglades.

There are many places in the park where people can enjoy watching birds.

Flamingos and other wading birds hunt for food in the Everglades.

an egret

Reptiles and Amphibians

Reptiles such as snakes, lizards, turtles, alligators and crocodiles all live in the Everglades. Reptiles are cold-blooded, so the warm weather of the Everglades makes it a perfect habitat for them. There are also many frogs that dwell in the Everglades, as well as other amphibians.

The Burmese python lives in the Everglades. It is one of the largest snakes on Earth. But the Everglades is not this snake's native, or natural, habitat. It is an **introduced** reptile that was accidentally released into the Everglades. The Burmese python feeds on birds and animals. This snake is considered to be a pest, because it eats the same animals as the natural **predators** in the park.

Think and Talk About ...

Park rangers of the Everglades are trying to remove Burmese pythons from the park. They have captured over 2000 of them, but many more remain.

a Burmese python

American tree frogs hide in a palm leaf.

Manatees and Panthers

The area in and around the Everglades is home to the very rare and unusual West Indian manatees. These animals are sometimes called "sea cows". Manatees are very heavy. They can weigh more than 1500 kilograms, and are really more closely related to elephants than to cows. Manatees swim in warm water of 20° C or more. Their thick, greyish skin is often wrinkled, which gives them a wise and gentle appearance. Manatees swim from fresh water to salt water and back again, so the Everglades is a perfect environment for them.
Rules are in place to make sure these amazing creatures are protected.

a West Indian manatee

Another extremely rare animal of the Everglades is the Florida panther. This large **carnivore** once lived all over south-eastern USA. Hunting has almost destroyed all the panthers and, today, there are fewer than 100 left in the wild. All of the remaining panthers live in and around the Everglades, protected by the national park. It is hoped that the protection will mean the number of panthers increases.

a Florida panther

Popular Activities at the Everglades

There are many exciting things to do in the Everglades. The most popular activity is looking for animals and birds. Visitors to the national park can walk along trails or walkways, or take a canoe ride along the water, to see wildlife. Rangers hold free guided nature walks and talks at areas where animals are likely to be seen.

Most people come to see the park's fascinating animals in the dry season. When most waterholes dry up, the animals gather at the few remaining ones. Many waterholes and animal viewing areas are near trails in areas such as Shark Valley and Royal Palm.

Visitors also like to use canoes or kayaks in the pools and rivers of the Everglades, and even on the ocean off its coast. By travelling on the water, people can see the animals up close in their natural habitat. There is also a 159-kilometre Wilderness Waterway with campsites that are located away from all park roads. Boat tours and tram tours are very popular, too. There are bike trails in the park as well.

Visitors enjoy paddling canoes in the Everglades.

Think and Talk About ...

More than one million people from all over the world visit the Everglades National Park each year.

Everglades Park Rangers

It is the job of the park rangers to look after the Everglades National Park. Some rangers are law-enforcement rangers. They patrol the park to make sure everyone obeys laws meant for visitor and animal safety. At the Everglades, speeding boats, water safety and animal encounters are the main concerns. Rangers give specific information on how visitors can stay safe near dangerous or poisonous animals. They can also assist in emergency rescues and the treatment of injured visitors.

Park rangers provide scientific, historical and general park information to visitors, too. They take visitors on guided tours and hikes. **Conservation groups** also help maintain the park's wilderness ecosystem.

Park rangers have an important job in the Everglades.

Protecting the Everglades

The Everglades is the largest subtropical wilderness in North America. It has one of the largest mangrove forests in the world. Within the Everglades, there are six threatened or **endangered** species of animals, including the American alligator, the American crocodile and the West Indian manatee.

The Everglades is the home of more wading birds than anywhere else in North America. Many migrating birds stop in the Everglades before continuing along their routes.

an American crocodile

For these reasons, the Everglades is recognised as a place that deserves special protection. In 1979, an international group of scientists listed the Everglades as a World Heritage Site.

The Everglades in Peril?

All the plants and animals in the Everglades depend on water. The Everglades is dependent on water from Lake Okeechobee – this is its main source of fresh water. But near the park are large cities with thousands of homes and businesses. These cities use the water from Lake Okeechobee, too. Farms surround the park as well, and also use water from the lake. In the past, a series of dams and canals was built to prevent flooding in the surrounding cities. The dams and canals channel water out of the park rather than through it, on the way to the ocean, so the Everglades receives less water.

Another water problem in the Everglades is pollution. **Fertilisers** and other chemicals have been found in the water, and these are harmful to the park's plants and animals.

The city of Coral Springs lies very close to the Everglades.

Taking Care of the Everglades

Visitors to the Everglades need to follow the rules that are in place for their safety and the protection of wildlife. When viewing wildlife, visitors are asked to stay on the specially marked trails and at a safe, recommended distance from the wildlife. Visitors are not allowed to touch the wildlife. If an animal seems to be injured, dangerous or is in a place where it may get hurt, visitors must immediately report this situation to a ranger. If visitors are taking a tour on a boat, they are asked to be aware of wildlife and stay a safe distance away. If a group is on a motor boat, it is very important to watch for animals that could be struck by the boat, and all speed limits must be maintained.

Signs in the park warn drivers to be careful not to hit panthers or other animals that are crossing the road.

PANTHER
TRAFFIC

On the Wilderness Waterway

by Maggie Alexander Graf (ten years old)

Last winter, my family and I spent a week in the Everglades for our vacation. We wanted to take a break from the cold weather up north and spend some time in the wilderness. Southern Florida is a lot warmer than New York City in January! After a few days of sightseeing by car, the final part of our trip was spent canoeing and camping for five days along the Everglades' "Wilderness Waterway".

Our journey was amazing and full of highlights. One thing that happened every day was bird spotting. We saw some birds in nests among bushes and small trees. Other birds were wading in the water or mud. And some flew above us – at times right over our heads! One cormorant plunged straight into the water and came out with a fish in its beak. I know it was a cormorant because we checked it in our bird identification book. We referred to that all the time.

a cormorant catching a fish

Seeing the animals of the Everglades up close was my favourite part of the trip. The animals I remember the most were the alligators that would **bask** along the shore, just sitting there absolutely still. They looked like statues. We only knew they were alive when they plopped into the water. I was nervous whenever an alligator glided alongside our boat. But they never bothered us at all.

Another incredible sighting was a huge manatee. We saw it swim right under us! We watched it for a while until it disappeared in the murky waters. We were also lucky enough to see the fins of dolphins sticking out of the water as they swam along. The Everglades was, as my mum said, "a feast for seeing large and unusual animals."

an alligator basking in shallow water

Sometimes, while we paddled in our boat, it seemed like we were in a maze of water surrounded by plants. And without any hills it was hard to know that we were going the right way. But the rangers of the Everglades had made it easy for us. There were signposts all along our route. A lot of the time, I spotted the signs among the trees and bushes before my parents did!

I think the final highlight for me was camping in the different campgrounds. My family has always enjoyed camping and we are used to putting up tents. In the Everglades we stayed at three kinds of campgrounds. One night, we had a regular campsite on the ground. Another night, we actually camped on the sand at the beach. That was especially nice because we built a fire and roasted marshmallows while watching the sunset. We had the beach all to ourselves. The other nights we stayed in "chickees". These are decks above the water where we set up our tent right on the wood. That was a new experience, and it was our favourite kind of campsite.

All in all it was a great trip, and I would recommend it to anyone!

a chickee

Glossary

bask (*verb*)	to lie in a warm place
carnivore (*noun*)	an animal that eats mostly meat
conservation groups (*noun*)	groups that work to protect areas of the natural world
descendants (*noun*)	all the people related to someone who lived long ago
distinct (*adjective*)	different from one another
ecosystem (*noun*)	a group of plants, animals and other organisms that rely on each other to survive
endangered (*adjective*)	having very few living members of the species left in the wild
fertilisers (*noun*)	chemicals to help crops grow
grassland (*noun*)	a large open area covered in grass
habitat (*noun*)	the natural home for a particular living thing
humid (*adjective*)	having lots of water vapour in the air
introduced (*adjective*)	brought to a place
limestone (*noun*)	rock made up of shells, coral and organic matter
predators (*noun*)	animals that eat particular other animals
subtropical (*adjective*)	almost as warm and humid as tropical climates
wading birds (*noun*)	long-legged birds that look for food in the water

Index